SUZY AND THE MOUSE KING

Hello from
Jan Wahl

Story by Jan Wahl

Illustrations by Catherine A. Macaro

Best wishes,
Catherine A. Macaro

Monroe County Library System
Monroe, Michigan 48161

Printed by the
Monroe County Library System
Graphic Services Department
Monroe, Michigan

October, 1992

To Sig, Sandy,
and Gaby
with love

J. W.

Suzy was frying fish. Each day she cooked — mended — cleaned the tiny cottage. Then she fished in the deep sea and cooked fish for her younger brothers and sisters.

**H**er brothers and sisters banged tin forks on the table. "We are hungry, *we are hungry!*"

The mother worked on a neighbor's farm and the father swept out the stable. They were very poor.

♥ ♥ ♥ ♥ ♥

When her father and mother came home supper lay ready. Sometimes, after all was done, she walked into town. There she could watch happy grown-ups dancing. SOMEDAY, thought Suzy, EVERYBODY WILL WATCH ME.

One day her father was angry. "No more going to town! It gives the girl ideas."

"I want to go where the stars are," Suzy sighed aloud.

**"Y**ou could stay home and knit, dear," suggested her mother. Yet Suzy sat by the window, gazing up at the stars. A constellation formed the letter S.

She looked her mother right in the eye. And her father too. "Otto is big and can take my place. I want to go out to work."

♥♥♥♥♥

Now they knew they could not stop her. Early next morning Suzy set off wearing her mended skirt and blouse. "I'll return with gifts for you," she called. The family stood lined up at the gate.

"Don't go far," her mother said wiping her eyes. Her father pretended a fish bone stuck in his throat.

"Goodbye!" yelled all her brothers and sisters.

When the town's church spire was far behind her, she came to a wide crossroads. "Which way makes my luck?"

♥ ♥ ♥ ♥ ♥

S uzy was about to throw chaff in the wind and go where it blew. Suddenly out from high, shiny ferns stepped a tall handsome young fellow dressed in green bright velvet.

♥ ♥ ♥ ♥ ♥

"Follow me, Suzy."

OH MY, thought Suzy. PRINCE CHARMING ALREADY. "I am looking for work," she said aloud.

"What luck!" replied the fine young man. "For I need somebody to look after my son, who has no mother."

Suzy clapped her hands. "This *is* luck!" Then she remembered her mother's words. "Is it far?"

♥♥♥♥♥

"**N**o, not far," he told her. So Suzy followed
♥♥♥♥♥ him down a long winding path through a
forest thick with leafy shrubs and they came to a loud
river where purple fog rolled. Up in the dark sky lots of
stars twinkled.

SO FAR SO GOOD, thought Suzy, HE IS PRINCE
CHARMING. HERE ARE MY STARS.

"Carry me," she said. At once the young man swung
Suzy up in his arms and waded into the water. After they
got to the other side she saw his suit was still dry.

♥♥♥♥♥

Though it must be night, here on the other side of the river it was broad daylight. They stood in a garden full of fresh lilies and tulips and clumps of pear trees. Wrens sang.

♥ ♥ ♥ ♥ ♥

B eyond the garden sat a high house with windows sparkling in the hot yellow sun. A little boy dressed in bright green velvet popped out of a hickory tree.

"Pa!" he shouted. "Is this my new ma?" "I am Suzy," she said.

"Ma!" squeaked the boy as if he hadn't heard her and she said: "I am not your mother." To herself: NOT YET.

♥ ♥ ♥ ♥ ♥

S uzy took his hand. She ran into the house with him. The boy's hand felt very cold. He had shiny black marvelous eyes like his father.

On the table supper lay ready. Cheese soup, cheese stew, ripe hunks of more cheese. After supper, the young man spoke.

♥♥♥♥♥

"**S**uzy! Each morning take my boy down to
♥♥♥♥♥ the old garden well. On a rock ledge sits a
jar of purple cream. Smear some on his eyes. But be
sure none of it EVER gets on yours."

"Yes Ma," added the boy. "Please listen to him."

Now the young man said, "And milk the brown cow.
You may have a mug to drink. Do anything you wish
after."

"That's all I must do?" Suzy asked.

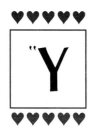**"Y**es. For this I will pay you with a gold coin each week."

"Terrific," she said. IT BEATS WORKING. After supper he gave Suzy a kiss on the forehead and went away. She tucked the boy in the bed next to hers.

"Give ME a kiss, Ma!" So she did.

♥♥♥♥♥

S uzy returned to the kitchen to wash dishes.
♥♥♥♥♥ They were clean. Tiny fuzzy things with long
tails slipped away. Suzy got goosebumps. "I must be
tired. I'll go to bed early. Tomorrow I will search."

And she crawled into her bed that was solid silver
hung with pink curtains. "If my family could see me!"
Before she knew it the boy shook her.

"WAKE UP, MA!" Suzy stretched and yawned, "Is it
morning?"

♥ ♥ ♥ ♥ ♥

While she had slept her old clothes had disappeared. Now she had a pretty silk dress and hot yellow satin shoes. What kind of house was this?

"Come!" coaxed the boy. She dressed him and herself and blinked at the gold mirror. HAVE I GROWN?

She ran through wet nicely clipped grass with the boy and they talked together. He was very smart for his age. He showed Suzy the well and the purple cream, which she smeared on his eyes. How large, how shiny black they became.

Suzy was about to dip her hand once again into the jar. "DON'T, MA!" The boy shivered like a leaf. "You will have to go away then. I don't want you to. I love you too much." And he hugged her tightly.

♥ ♥ ♥ ♥ ♥

S oon Suzy found the magnificent brown cow and a low stool and a pail and she milked the cow. The little boy shared the tin mug with her.

Then without a word he whizzed off past the pear trees and left Suzy alone. She ambled to the high house just in time to spy those quick tails again disappearing into a tiny hole in the wall!

♥ ♥ ♥ ♥ ♥

Suzy was sure she heard squeaks. And whispers. The kitchen was clean and spotless. "I almost wish I was cooking for my brothers and sisters. There is nothing to do here."

She started to hunt about in the cupboards. At last in a kitchen corner sat a basket with a note on it. *I AM SUZY'S,* it said.

♥ ♥ ♥ ♥ ♥

In the basket lay balls of fluffy yarn and shiny knitting needles. She thought of her family, missing them. "I will knit sweaters to take back with me."

So Suzy picked out her favorite colors of yarn and began. As needles clicked to and fro, queer music played. If Suzy stopped, the music did too!

**T**hat night at supper she asked, "*Who* plays music? *Who* sets our table? *Where* do you go?"

Groaning, the young man's jaw sank and he put down his napkin. "Suzy, do not ask!" He leaned over and gave her a kiss. "Sleep well." WHO CAN SLEEP?

 **E**ach morning after Suzy and the boy got up, they went to the well. After sharing their mug of milk, the boy raced off after reminding her:

"Thanks, Ma. Never put the cream on your own eyes!"

Away he ran beyond the pear trees and Suzy went to the house to knit. What else? The house always lay spotless. Never a cobweb! Later the table set itself. That queer music made her wish to dance.

♥ ♥ ♥ ♥ ♥

S o, remembering dances in town, Suzy would dance by herself. It was not the same as dancing along with a fine suitor, of course.

♥ ♥ ♥ ♥ ♥

**O**ne day she picked a bunch of pussywillows from the creek. She arranged it in a vase. It reminded her of cats standing by her parents' door hoping for fishbones. "May I have a *cat* for company?" Suzy asked later. "I won't be so lonely."

Both the boy and his father screamed.

"We are allergic to cats!" exclaimed the young man — shuddering. Suzy had made some cat drawings. The boy tore them up in terror. This was the end of that!

ne afternoon Suzy studied the piles of knitting behind her. HOW LONG HAVE I BEEN HERE? WEEKS OR YEARS? She walked to her room and glanced into the gold mirror.

I AM TALLER, FILLING OUT MY DRESS. SOON I WILL BE A WOMAN. THE YOUNG MAN MAY WANT TO MARRY ME. BUT WHERE DOES HE GO?

♥ ♥ ♥ ♥ ♥

S oft whisker shadows scuttled down the hall
♥ ♥ ♥ ♥ ♥ as Suzy rushed back to the garden. "I must
see what happens. I will rub purple cream on my eyes."

It stung. Suzy bent over — cooling her smarting eyes
with water from the well. The water cleared. Down deep
lay a wee crystal palace. Busy furry mice with pointy
ears hurried in and out. In and out.

**A**mong them strutted a mouse wearing bright green velvet. On his head sat a crown shining with seed pearls. On one paw he wore a ruby. Just like the young man's ring. PRINCE CHARMING WAS THE KING OF MICE!

"I think I'm going to be sick!" moaned Suzy.

She turned to glance behind her. The garden was full of singing mice. Working with wheelbarrows and rakes and hoes.

In the middle played a very tiny one in a grass green outfit. Suzy buttoned those same clothes on him that morning!

♥♥♥♥♥

For the rest of the day Suzy did not knit. She sat
♥♥♥♥♥ numb. At supper time, the handsome young
fellow came in, joking and whistling with his son. It was
hard for Suzy to swallow her cheese.

"Something wrong?" asked the young man. "Oh no," said
Suzy. But as he kissed her good night she was sure she
smelled mouse breath.

That night Suzy did not sleep a wink. Tossing and turning.
At midnight the music began! Suzy climbed out of bed
to follow. The boy watched her from his bed. And she
sped along the halls of the house until she reached a
small oak door.

She bent down low to peek through the keyhole into a
huge room brilliant with light. Mice musicians played
horns and tiny fiddles. On the bass drum it said, "The
Rodents."

♥♥♥♥♥

F rom a door on the wall opposite out sprang
♥♥♥♥♥ the Mouse King. He led a group of elegantly
dressed mice. He asked one attractive girl mouse to
dance.

The two danced quite close — dipping and gliding —
silently gazing into each other's dark round eyes.

Suzy's heart thump! thump! bumped. Quickly she dashed
back to bed. And sobbed:

"I am a silly GIRL
wishing to be a WOMAN!
I live in a scary
HOUSE
with Prince Charming
who is really a
MOUSE!"

**H**ow she missed her big, noisy family. The little boy watched her from under his blanket and put his fist over his mouth.

He wept also, until he fell asleep.

♥ ♥ ♥ ♥ ♥

T he next morning, the tall handsome young man got ready to depart again. Suzy stamped her foot. "Go *back* to your disgusting mice!"

♥ ♥ ♥ ♥ ♥

His face drooped and he twitched.

"Girl! Why did you do it? You have SEEN things you should not have. Now we must part forever. Come!" Suzy did not cry. Calmly, she gathered up all her wool knitting.

And she kissed the little boy who stood under the pear tree. His nose felt cold. "Pa will never catch a Ma like you again. I wish you could stay with us," he pleaded. His voice rose to a squeak.

His boy ears became mouse ears . . . a mouse tail started sprouting. Since the truth was out, purple cream was not necessary.

The boy waved. As Suzy waved back, pears plopped from the tree boughs and the ground began to rumble.

♥♥♥♥♥

As fast as he could, the boy's father, the young man, pulled her toward the bank of the loud river with the thick rolling purple fog. He became smaller. Slipperier.

Trying to forget he was only a gray-brown mouse, Suzy clung close to him. Her bundle of sweaters dragged along as he rapidly swam across the swirling river. He swam faster.

Of course the wool got drenched and smelled horrible. Suzy's sweaters shrank. "Put these on your mice," she snapped as soon as they reached the other side. "I can't use them!"

Long faced, the young man said nothing. He stood only as tall as her waist now.

♥ ♥ ♥ ♥ ♥

Suzy shut her eyes tight in horror. She did not dare to see his face change. After she opened them, it was night. Not day. Her beautiful dress and shoes were gone and she was wearing her old patched clothes.

Something, however, glowed at her feet — a purse!

In it lay a gold coin for each week and this made a lot more than she remembered.

♥♥♥♥♥

S linging the purse over her back, she stumbled
♥♥♥♥♥ home through thick and sharp brambles and
briars. At last Suzy found the cottage. It needed paint.
Her family was just rising out of their straw cots as
she stepped through the door.

Her brother Otto was already preparing hot porridge
for breakfast. How tall and pale she was. At first, not
even Otto recognized her.

"I am your lost daughter!" Suzy yelled to her parents
who stared at her, open-mouthed.

ondering, "Do you believe it?" she sat down weakly. And sobbed:

"I was a silly GIRL
hoping to be a WOMAN!
I lived in a scary
HOUSE
with Prince Charming
who was really a
MOUSE!"

Her family smirked and roared and giggled.

"Girl, we can't believe that. No sir!" Not even when she showed them her purse bulging with gold coins did they believe her.

"She suffered sunstroke," said her mother.

"She needs porridge," said her father. Anyhow, with the coins she had earned, Suzy paid for a nice farm for her father, and for her mother she bought a cow plus a spotted hen to lay a big, brown egg each day.

Suzy felt she did not belong at home any longer. She spent many hours by herself, fishing.

One pleasant, sunny afternoon a bold young fisher lad tossed a wide net at the deep blue sea. It got stuck and he waded in to free it.

"Here, let *me* help!" called Suzy so help she did. The fisher lad smelled like freshly caught fish and new wind and brine.

Suzy raced him down a sandy shell-strewn beach. Finally they stopped and happened to look at each other. His eyes sparkled blue-green as the mysterious color of sea in low sun.

Every afternoon Suzy came to help pull the net. The two would pull — and yank — together. His name was Erik.

♥ ♥ ♥ ♥ ♥

n Suzy's wedding day her patched dress was gone and there in its place hung a gown of whitest satin a-glitter with twinkling stars. The magic stars were sewn in S's.

♥♥♥♥♥

♥♥♥♥♥ hen Suzy walked off to church to marry that fisher lad, three hundred mice held her long proud train. The ring bearer was the mouse son. The very sad King of Mice stayed home.

He sent a note: *I wish you*
a lucky life.
I wish you
were my wife.

"We believe you!" shouted her family.